CIRRUS CLOUDS

B. Taurus: **BESSIE**

H. Sapiens: **BAILEY**

TORNADO ALLEY

INCLUDES TX, OK, KS, NE, SD although TWISTERS OCCUR throughout NORTH AMERICA and the world

FUJITA scale
RATES TORNADO INTENSITY

F0 40-72mph GALE

F1 73-112mph MODERATE

F2 113-157mph CONSIDERABLE

F3 158-206mph EXTREME

F4 207-260mph DEVASTATING

F5 261-318mph INCREDIBLE

F6 319-375mph INCONCEIVABLE

For Ma and Pa,
With a tip o' the hat to the Bozeman Writers Group.
C. F.

THIS IS A BORZOI BOOK PUBLISHED BY ALFRED A. KNOPF

Published in the United States of America by Alfred A. Knopf,
a division of Random House, Inc., New York,
and simultaneously in Canada by Random House of Canada Limited, Toronto.

Distributed by Random House, Inc., New York.

Knopf, Borzoi Books, and the colophon are registered trademarks of Random House, Inc.

www.randomhouse.com/kids   www.carolynfisher.com

Library of Congress Cataloging-in-Publication Data

Fisher, Carolyn, 1968–
A Twisted Tale / by Carolyn Fisher
p.   cm.
Summary: After a tornado hits Bailey Tarbell's family farm,
all the animals are mixed up and it takes some creative thinking
for Bailey to get things straightened out—almost!
ISBN 0-375-81540-6 (trade) – ISBN 0-375-91540-0 (lib. bdg.)
[1. Domestic animals–Fiction. 2. Tornadoes–Fiction.
3. Humorous stories.]
I. Title.
PZ7.F4994 Tw 2002
[E]–dc21

Printed in the United States of America
May 2002
10 9 8 7 6 5 4 3 2 1

A Twisted Tale

BY CAROLYN FISHER

Alfred A. Knopf • New York

BAILEY TARBELL lived on a FARM

with

her ma,

her pa...

...a cow,

moo

a cat,

a dog,

meow

Arf

cluck

cluck

cluck

a duck, quack

three chickens,

AND a pig.

One day, a sudden gust of wind blew up from the west. Bailey glanced at the sky. "Yippety-yodle-eye-hay, there's a twister coming!" she cried.

Quick as spit, Bailey herded the animals into the barn. Then she ran down to the storm cellar with Ma and Pa.

The wind howled like a prom queen steppin' on a cow patty.

It tore the roof right off the barn and whirled those animals into the air.

The cow's eyes bulged.

The cat's fur

The pig's knuckles turned white.

Stood on end.

Then that twister
spat out the critters
like a cowpoke spits out
a wad of chew.

When the wind blew away,

Bailey burst out of the storm cellar just in time

to see the cow fly over to the chicken coop

and sit on the nests. "Cluck, cluck!" she squawked.

"Quack, quack!" rasped the pig.

She dove into the pond.

The cat chased the dog, who climbed up a tree and yowled. "Well, I'll be hornswoggled!" cried Bailey.

"The twister mixed up the animals."

ccccluckacluckacluck

"Jumpin' Jehoshaphat!" Pa said.
"What are we going to do?"
Bailey said, "Let's call the vet."

So Ma phoned Doc Smoot, who looked at
the animals and scratched his chin.
"It's plumb peculiar!" Doc Smoot said.
He took their temperatures.
He peered into their ears.
He fed them large red pills.
But nothing changed. Doc
Smoot shrugged and went away.

Bailey did everything she could to cure the animals.
She demonstrated animal behavior.
(Ma and Pa helped.)

Bailey even tried hypnosis.

Nothing Worked.

Bailey was baffled. Meanwhile, the cow perched on the roof and CROWED.

The chickens **rooted** in the

MUD.

The cat gnawed a bone,
the dog chased **mice**,
and the pig
was as **wrinkled**
as a raisin.

Then one day, as Bailey got out of her bath, she twirled a towel around her head and watched the water SWIRL down the drain.

"Eureka!" she cried. "That's it."

She told Ma and Pa her plan. They loaded the animals into the truck and drove to the nearest...

...Carnival.

They screamed through the Scrambler.

They flew on the Ferris Wheel.
They crashed through the **Cannonball.**
But they were still mixed up.

Then Bailey saw a ride
that was **bigger** than the rest.
"Why, I'll be hopped!"
Bailey said. "It's the Twister!"

"QUACK, QUACK!" rasped the duck.

"OINK, OINK!" squealed the pig.

"cluck, cluck!" cried the chickens.

When the Twister
jolted to a stop,

Bailey and the animals

stumbled back to the truck.

As Pa drove home, they listened to the right sounds coming from the cow, the cat, the dog, the duck, three chickens, and a pig.

meeooooowW

quackquack

Ooink pinkpink cluck cluckcluck

cluckcluckcluck CLUCKCLUCK

CLUCKCLUCKCLUCK

MOOOOOOo

"Ooo-wee," said Pa, "it's good to be back to normal."

"Ooo-wee," said Ma, "Bailey, you are somethin' clever."

But Bailey said, "WEE-OOOOO!"

TWISTER

HEIGHT
8 miles

RIDE TIME
9.6 MINUTES

TYPE COASTER
of
hyper INVERTED
multi-element

3000 ft DROP

TOP 200
SPEED
m.p.h.

3600°
HELIX

26 mile
CIRCUIT

ACCELERATION:
0-80 mph in 1.8 seconds

H. Sapiens: **BAILEY**

S. Scrofa: **WILBUR**

B. Taurus: **BESSIE**

negative G's